VISIT US AT
www.abdopublishing.com

Reinforced library bound edition published in 2010 by Spotlight, a division of the ABDO Group, 8000 West 78th Street, Edina, Minnesota 55439. Spotlight produces high-quality reinforced library bound editions for schools and libraries. Published by agreement with Warner Bros.—A Time Warner Company. All rights reserved. Used under authorization.

Printed in the United States of America, Melrose Park, Illinois.
092009
012010

 PRINTED ON RECYCLED PAPER

Library of Congress Cataloging-in-Publication Data

Busch, Robbie.
  Scooby-Doo in Don't play dummy with me! / writer, Robbie Busch ; penciller, Vincent Deporter ; inker, Horacio Ottolini ; colorist, Paul Becton ; letterer, Tom Orzechowski. -- Reinforced library bound ed.
     p. cm. -- (Scooby-Doo graphic novels)
  ISBN 978-1-59961-693-3
  I. DePorter, Vince. II. Scooby-Doo (Television program) III. Title. IV. Title: Don't play dummy with me!
  PZ7.7.B9Sd 2010
  741.5'973--dc22

                          2009032898

All Spotlight books have reinforced library bindings and
are manufactured in the United States of America.

SOMEBODY MADE OFF WITH ALL MY *PAYROLL MONEY*. THE FUTURE OF MY *TRAVELLING CIRCUS* WAS IN THAT SAFE! AND ON TOP OF THAT, MY *STAR ATTRACTION* DISAPPEARS!

WHEN DID SAL LASPARIE DISAPPEAR, MR. McLOONEY?

MAYBE *HE* STOLE THE MONEY AND *RAN AWAY?*

LAST TIME ANYONE SAW SAL WAS SOMEWHERES BETWEEN *HERE* AND OUR *LAST* CITY. I KNOW HE DIDN'T TAKE THE MONEY AND RUN-- HE *COULDN'T* HAVE!

ER-- WHY IS THAT?

WELL, FIRST OFF, 'CAUSE HE DIDN'T HAVE NO *LEGS*. HE'S THE *LEGLESS VENTRILOQUIST*-- THAT'S HIS *CLAIM* TO *FAME!*

AND THE *SECOND* REASON?

Don't play DUMMY with me!

SECOND REASON IS, HE LEFT HIS *PARTNER* BEHIND-- AND HE WOULDN'T HAVE GONE NOWHERE WITHOUT *BORIS!*

Sal & Boris TONIGHT!

ROBBIE BUSCH - WRITER
VINCENT DEPORTER - ARTIST
TOM ORZECHOWSKI - LETTERER
PAUL BECTON - COLORIST
DIGITAL CHAMELEON - SEPARATIONS
HARVEY RICHARDS - ASSISTANT EDITOR
JOAN HILTY - EDITOR

THEY WAS *CONNECTED...* YA KNOW WHAT I MEAN?

SO, YOU DON'T THINK HE WAS INVOLVED IN THE ROBBERY?

HE WAS AN ODD DUCK--BUT HE WAS A HARD-WORKIN', HONEST MAN.

AND I KNOW HE COULDN'T SURVIVE WITHOUT BORIS. THEY WAS LIKE TWO PARTS OF THE SAME PERSON.

THAT MAY BE, BUT WE CAN'T RULE OUT ANY SUSPECTS JUST YET.

AND WE'LL HAVE TO TALK TO *ALL* OF YOUR EMPLOYEES.

LIKE, CAN I SEE BORIS? I'M PRETTY GOOD AT THROWING MY VOICE!

NO! HE'S A FRAGILE PIECE OF EQUIPMENT, NOT A *TOY!*

LIKE, SORRY, MAN!

THAT'S ALL RIGHT, SON... I GUESS WE'VE JUST COME TO THINK OF BORIS AS A PART OF THE FAMILY.

SNIFF SNIFF

RIKES!

RET ME OUTTA RERE!

CRASH!!

HEY-- OOF!

RUH-ROH!

SORRY ABOUT THAT-- SCOOBY GETS A LITTLE *OVEREXCITED* SOMETIMES.

HUMPH! *WHAT* ARE YOU CHILDREN DOING BACK HERE?!

WELL, BECAUSE...

THEY'RE HERE BECAUSE I *ASKED* 'EM TO BE, MERTRON!

I SEE YOU HAVE THAT UGLY WOODEN *MONSTER!*

TOO BAD HIS DADDY DIDN'T *TAKE* HIM WHEN HE *ROLLED AWAY* FROM HERE!

THE
END

OVER A THOUSAND YEARS AGO, THE EMPEROR OF CHINA POSSESSED A MYSTERIOUS GLOWING GREEN STONE, FILLED WITH GREAT POWER, CALLED **THE DRAGON'S EYE.**

THE EMPEROR CUT THE STONE INTO SEVEN INTERLOCKING STONES, WHICH HE DISTRIBUTED AMONG HIS SONS. OVER TIME, THE STONES WERE SCATTERED AROUND THE WORLD.

A MYSTERIOUS VILLAIN NAMED **LEE SHIU SHIAN** HAS STOLEN ALL OF THESE STONES, BEATING THE MEMBERS OF **MYSTERY INC.** AT EVERY TURN. NOW, WITH THE HELP OF TWO POLICE OFFICIALS, THE TEEN SLEUTHS HOPE TO CATCH LEE BEFORE HE CAN REASSEMBLE THE DRAGON'S EYE, BUT TIME IS **RUNNING OUT...**

HONG KONG.

LEE SHIU SHIAN MUST HAVE GONE STRAIGHT FROM BEIJING TO WHEREVER HE'S TAKING THE DRAGON'S EYE.

MAYBE HE LEFT BEHIND A CLUE?

WE'RE TOO LATE. HE'S *GONE!*

LIKE, THIS PLACE IS *HUGE.* OUR VILLAIN MUST BE *LOADED!*

SURE. HE HAD TO FINANCE ALL THOSE *AROUND-THE-WORLD THEFTS!*

YOU KNOW WHAT I ALWAYS SAY: "THE BIGGER THE *HOME...*"

...REE RETTER REE RITCHEN!

SO LET'S *CHECK OUT* THAT *KITCHEN!*

LEE SHIU SHIAN'S A VERY SUCCESSFUL BUSINESS-MAN.

SO WHY DOES HE HAVE ALL THESE *GEOLOGIST'S TOOLS*, OFFICER CHEUNG?

HIS *FATHER* WAS A GEOLOGIST AND ARCHAEOLOGIST. LEE PROBABLY LEARNED ABOUT THE DRAGON'S EYE FROM HIM.

THEN HE MAY HAVE TAKEN THE COMPONENTS OF THE DRAGON'S EYE TO ONE OF THE *SITES* IN THESE PHOTOS-- BUT *WHICH ONE?*

IS ONE OF THEM NAMED *KWAIDOON?*

HOW DID YOU KNOW?

LIKE, THERE'S A *ROUTE* TO IT MARKED ON THIS *MAP.*

I CAN'T READ CHINESE, BUT THESE LOOK LIKE *AIRLINE TICKET RECEIPTS*, TOO. THEY WERE ALL UNDER A MAGNET ON THE *FRIDGE!*

I CAN'T BELIEVE IT...

WHAT? THERE'S ENOUGH FOR THE REST OF YOU.

...SHAGGY'S AND SCOOBY'S CONSTANT ESCAPES TO THE KITCHEN FINALLY *PAID OFF!*

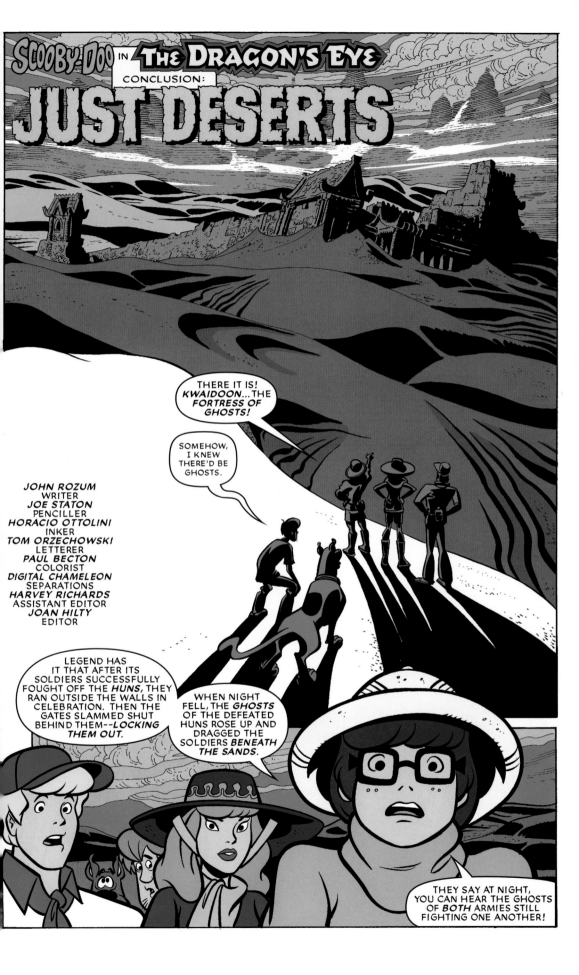

W-WE SHOULD JUST LEAVE THEM TO IT AND *G-GO HOME!*

RELAX, SHAGGY. THAT'S JUST A *LEGEND*. THERE *AREN'T* ANY GHOSTS.

THEN WHAT DO YOU CALL *THOSE?*

CALL *WHAT,* SHAGGY? THERE'S NOTHING THERE!

AND THAT *WAILING* IS JUST THE DESERT WIND.

LIKE, I DIDN'T SAY I *HEARD* A GHOST. I SAID I *SAW* ONE-- ACTUALLY, *TWO!*

RHERE ROES RANOTHER RUN!

WHERE?

THERE. THERE. THERE.

AND...uh... THERE.

SO, WE MEET AT *LAST*. FACE TO FACE, WITH NO DISGUISES BETWEEN US.

YOU KIDS ARE VERY *PERSISTENT*, I'LL GIVE YOU THAT.

I ALMOST HAD TO WORK HARD TO OBTAIN THE LAST FEW COMPONENTS OF THE *DRAGON'S EYE*.

YOU WERE WORTHY OPPONENTS, BUT AS YOU WELL KNOW...

...I NOW HAVE THE *ENTIRE JEWEL*. YOU KNOW WHAT *THAT* MEANS, DON'T YOU?

I *WIN*.

IT'S *NOT* OVER YET!

IT *IS* OVER-- FOR *YOU*.

‹TIE THEM UP!›*

*MANDARIN CHINESE.

CRINKLE

WHAT DO YOU HOPE TO ACCOMPLISH WITH THE DRAGON'S EYE? IT'S JUST A *STONE*.

HARDLY! OTHERWISE I WOULDN'T HAVE GONE TO SO MUCH *TROUBLE* TO OBTAIN IT!

THE DRAGON'S EYE CONTAINS *IMMENSE POWER*. ONCE IT IS REASSEMBLED, THAT POWER WILL BE MINE TO CONTROL.

"YOU KNOW THE LEGEND. THE DESERT OUTSIDE THIS FORTRESS HAS SWALLOWED UP THE BONES OF *THOUSANDS* OF ANCIENT WARRIORS.

"THE *FIRST* THING I WILL DO IS CALL THEM UP OUT OF THEIR GRAVES, AND ASSEMBLE THEM INTO THE *GREATEST AND MOST TERRIFYING ARMY* THE WORLD HAS EVER SEEN!

"THEN, I WILL USE THAT ARMY TO *RECLAIM* CHINA FROM THOSE WHO HAVE LET IT FADE FROM POWER.

CHINA

"WITH CHINA STRONG AGAIN, I WILL SEND MY ARMIES OUT INTO THE SURROUNDING COUNTRIES, CONQUERING THEM ONE BY ONE, UNTIL..."

...THE ENTIRE *WORLD* IS MINE TO COMMAND!

YOU DON'T ACTUALLY *BELIEVE* THAT NONSENSE?

"...WHAT DO YOU HOPE TO ACCOMPLISH WITH *THAT?*"

BEHOLD!

GRAB!

!

LIKE I SAID-- IT'S *NOT* OVER YET!

YOU DON'T ACTUALLY THINK YOU'LL *ESCAPE*, DO YOU?!

AFTER HIM!

YAY, FREDDIE!

SHUCKS, YOU *CAUGHT* ME.

HERE YOU GO!

YES! YES!

WHO WOULD DARE USE THE POWER OF THE DRAGON'S EYE FOR ILL INTENT?

LOOK, LIKE, THESE "GHOSTS" WHO TIED US UP MIGHT NOT BE REAL, BUT THAT ONE LOOKS PLENTY REAL TO *ME*!

REE TOO!

‹LOOK! IT'S THE ANCIENT EMPEROR HIMSELF!›

ARE YOU THE FOOLISH ONE, LEE SHIU SHIAN?

DON'T JUST STAND THERE, YOU *FOOLS*! GET HIM!

IT'S A *REAL* GHOST! RUN!